iVy + BEAN

BOOK 11

MORE THAN 5 MILLION COPIES SOLD!

* An ALA Notable Children's Book

* A Booklist Editors' Choice

* A Kirkus Reviews Best Book of the Year

* A Book Links Best New Book for the Classroom

* A New York Public Library Title for Reading and Sharing

* A *People* magazine's "Summer's Hottest Reads" selection

ivy + BEAN

ONE BIG HAPPY FAMILY

BOOK 11

written by annie barrows + illustrated by sophie blackall

chronicle books · san francisco

For Sara Gillingham,
without whom this would be a pile of scribbles.
—A. B. + S. B.

Text © 2018 by Annie Barrows.
Illustrations © 2018 by Sophie Blackall.

Library of Congress Cataloging-in-Publication Data:

Names: Barrows, Annie, author. I Blackall, Sophie, illustrator. I Barrows, Annie.
Ivy + Bean (Series) ; bk. 11.
Title: Ivy + Bean : one big happy family / written by Annie Barrows ;
illustrated by Sophie Blackall.
Other titles: One big happy family
Description: San Francisco : Chronicle Books, [2018] I Series: Ivy + Bean ;
book 11 I Summary: When classmate Vanessa insists that all single children are spoiled,
Ivy wonders whether she can become "unspoiled" by giving away all her clothes at
school (which does not go over well with her teacher or parents)—but ultimately
decides that all she needs to accomplish her goal is a little sister.
Identifiers: LCCN 2017046554 I ISBN 9781452164007 (alk. paper)
Subjects: LCSH: Ivy (Fictitious character : Barrows)—Juvenile fiction.
I Bean (Fictitious character : Barrows)—Juvenile fiction. I Only child—Juvenile fiction.
I Sisters—Juvenile fiction. I Best friends—Juvenile fiction. I CYAC: Family life—Fiction.
I Only child—Fiction. I Sisters—Fiction. I Best friends—Fiction. I Friendship—Fiction.,
Classification: LCC PZ7.B27576 Iwbgh 2018 I DDC 813.6 [Fic] —dc23 LC record
available at https://lccn.loc.gov/2017046554

ISBN 978-1-4521-6400-7

Manufactured in China.

Book design by Sara Gillingham Studio.
Typeset in Blockhead and Candida.
The illustrations in this book were rendered in Chinese ink.

10 9 8 7 6 5 4 3 2 1

Chronicle Books LLC
680 Second Street, San Francisco, California 94107

Chronicle Books—we see things differently.
Become part of our community at www.chroniclekids.com.

CONTENTS

IMPORTANT PEOPLE, IMPORTANT GORILLAS 7

TOO CLOTHES FOR COMFORT 20

HELP MUH! 34

THE ROAD TO DISASTERVILLE 44

IN A PIGGLE 58

ASKING FOR TROUBLE 68

MIRACLE IN MONKEY PARK 83

NOT TOO BIG, NOT TOO LITTLE 95

A KNOTTY PROBLEM 108

BLOOP, BLOOP, BLOOP 114

IMPORTANT PEOPLE, IMPORTANT GORILLAS

"My Important People," wrote Bean at the top of her paper. Whew! Seventeen letters! Time for a break.

"Bean," said Ms. Aruba-Tate. "Do you need help?"

"I'm resting," explained Bean.

"Nobody else is resting," Vanessa said. Her table was next-door to Bean's. She was already drawing pictures of her Important People.

My Important people

Mom

Dad

"Thank you, Vanessa," said Ms. Aruba-Tate, in a way that really meant, Stop talking. Then she said "Bean" in a way that really meant, Get to work.

Bean sighed and picked up her pencil. My Important People. Okie-dokie, line 'em up. She drew her mom. She drew her mom eating a whole cake by herself. Her mom liked cake.

"Mom," she wrote. Then she drew her dad, with a wooden spoon. He was making more cake for her mom. "Dad," she wrote. Bean scrunched her older sister, Nancy, down in a corner. She drew some flies buzzing around her head. "Nancy," she wrote.

Bean looked around the classroom. Every-one was drawing like crazy. Eric was drawing so hard his tongue was hanging out. Marga-Lee had made frames around each of her Important People. Bean wished she'd thought of that.

She went back to drawing. Grandma. Grandpa. Other Grandpa. Two uncles. Three aunts. Four cousins. One cousin who wasn't a real cousin, but Bean liked him a lot anyway. He had a pet alligator. Bean put the alligator in there, too. Cool! Now Ivy.

"You should be finishing up, friends," said Ms. Aruba-Tate.

"I haven't put in my cousins yet!" yelled Emma.

"I haven't even finished my brothers and sisters!" yelled Vanessa.

Everyone scribble-scrabbled as fast as they could. Bean peeked over at Ivy's paper to see if she had included Bean. She had! Bean peeked some more. Ivy had drawn her mom, her grandma, her aunt, Bean, Abraham Lincoln, Mary Anning, Boudicca, and a gorilla. Wow, thought Bean. Abraham Lincoln! Bean wanted to copycat, but she didn't. She drew

Ms. Aruba-Tate instead. Ms. Aruba-Tate was as good as Abraham Lincoln any day!

+ + + + + +

When they were done, Ms. Aruba-Tate pinned their Important People on the art wall. She was decorating for Open House. Open House was when the grown-ups came to school to see what their kids had been doing all year, and Ms. Aruba-Tate said she wanted the classroom to look fantabulous. Everyone helped. Dusit and Drew picked fuzz-balls out of the carpet. Ivy turned all the books the right way on the bookshelf.

Emma and
Marga-Lee
swept the floor.
Bean blew the
extra glitter
down the heater
vent. Eric made sure
there was no yucky old
food in the lunchbox cubbies. Zuzu scraped
glue off the tables with her fingernails.
Vanessa said she was cleaning pencil boxes,
but really, she was standing at the art wall,
checking out everyone's Important People.

"Ivy," she called. "You can't have a gorilla
be one of your Important People."

Ivy sat back on her heels. "Why not?"

"Because a gorilla isn't a person!" said Vanessa. "You're supposed to draw people. People in your family!"

"Gorillas are in our family," said Ivy. "People and gorillas are related."

"Yeah!" said Bean. "Look at Tarzan."

"But that's not what it's supposed to be," Vanessa argued. "You're supposed to draw people like your brothers and sisters. Look at mine!" She pointed to hcr Important People. There were two brothers and three sisters, arranged in order of importance. "You're not supposed to draw gorillas! Or Abraham Lincoln!"

If there was one thing Bean couldn't stand, it was a bossy-buttons. "You're just jealous because you didn't think of Abraham Lincoln! Or a gorilla!"

"I am not!" snapped Vanessa. "I already have lots of Important People, right in my real family."

"Vanessa and Bean," said Ms. Aruba-Tate. "Why don't you agree to disagree and move away from each other? Ivy's Important People can be anyone—or any gorilla—she chooses."

"See?" said Bean to Vanessa.

"Bean," said Ms. Aruba-Tate, "will you help me make a sign that says 'Our Art Gallery'? I'll write out the words for you to copy."

"Sure, Ms. Aruba-Tate," said Bean. She tried not

to smile ha-ha at Vanessa, but she couldn't help it.

Vanessa stomped away.

+ + + + + +

By the time the bell rang, the second-graders were worn to a nubbin. "Good work, friends," said Ms. Aruba-Tate, looking around. "This classroom looks fantabulous!" It did, too.

"I'm beat," said Eric as he came out into the breezeway. He fell onto a bench.

"I'm bushed," said Dusit. He fell on the bench, too.

"I'm fainting," said Zuzu. She fainted into a planter.

"I'm pooped!" said Bean. She crumpled to her knees in the middle of the breezeway. "I have to crawl home."

"Me too," said Ivy, crumpling alongside Bean. "I've never cleaned that hard in my whole life."

"That's because you're an only child," said Vanessa's voice, high above them. "I have to clean all the time at home. And cook, too. And take care of my brothers and sisters. So I'm used to it." She gave a big sigh. "Only children never do any work. That's why they're usually spoiled."

Bean could have bitten Vanessa on the ankle, but she didn't. She just said, "Ivy's not spoiled."

"I know this kid who's totally spoiled," said Eric. "If you don't do what he says, he screams."

"My cousin Ryanne is so spoiled," said Zuzu, "she won't let you play with anything. She'll bring out one old toy and that's all you can play with. She hides everything else and says she lost it."

"My brother knows this guy who's so spoiled, he yells at his mom," said Dusit. "He yells, 'Go get me a pizza! Right now!'"

"And she does?" asked Eric.

Dusit nodded.

"Wow," said Eric. "I'd get sent to my room for a hundred years."

"Sometimes," said Dusit, "he yells so much his mom lets him drive the car."

"No way!" said Bean.

"Yes way!" Dusit nodded.

"That's nutso," said Bean. She looked up at Vanessa. "Ivy isn't like that."

"I didn't say she was!" Vanessa argued. "I just said that only children are usually spoiled."

"Well, Ivy's not," said Bean. "Are you, Ivy?"

Ivy rolled over on her back and looked up at Vanessa. "Well . . ." Suddenly, her arms shivered.

Bean frowned.

"I think I might be," Ivy said in a squeaky voice. Now her legs quivered. "I feel it coming on. Right now!"

Bean started smiling. "Oh no! She's spoiling!"

"It's happening! Here it comes!" Ivy wiggled all over. "I can't help it!"

"Try to hold it in!" called Eric.

But it was too late.

"GET ME A PIZZA!" yelled Ivy. "OR ELSE!"

TOO CLOTHES
FOR COMFORT

Luckily, Ivy recovered quickly. All they had to do was sprinkle a little water on her face. At first it didn't help, but after Rose the Yard Duty told them to stop pouring water all over the breezeway, Ivy said she felt normal enough to walk home.

"That was a close call," she said. "I still feel a little spoiled."

"We have to cure you," Bean agreed. "Of your terrible spoilment."

"We'd better do it soon," said Ivy.

But when they got to Bean's house, it was more fun to play spoiled child. Of course, they didn't yell at Bean's dad. They just yelled at each other. First Bean was spoiled, and Ivy was the mom. Then Ivy was spoiled, and Bean was the mom. In the end, they were both spoiled, and they put Bean's old toy car on top of her trampoline and jumped inside it, until Bean's dad came outside and told them to stop acting like crazy people. Then Ivy went home, and Bean drew six pictures with frames around them, and, with one thing and another, she forgot all about Ivy being spoiled. Even Ivy forgot about it, until the next morning.

Ivy and Bean almost always walked to school together. Ivy was almost always ready before Bean, so she almost always waited for Bean on the sidewalk.

Bean ran out her front door. "Forgot my lunch!" she hollered and ran back inside.

Bean ran out her front door. "Just a sec!" she hollered and ran back inside.

Bean ran out her front door. This time she got to the sidewalk. She stopped and stared at Ivy. "Are you cold?"

"No," said Ivy. "I'm hot."

"Why are you wearing two coats?" asked Bean.

"And three sweaters. And two dresses," added Ivy. "Because I'm going to give them away. So I won't be spoiled. You want a coat?"

"No thank you," said Bean. She already had a coat. "You're walking really slow."

"I can't bend my knees," Ivy explained. "I'm wearing three pairs of tights."

They were a little late to school.

+ + + + + +

By the end of lunch, Ivy had given away both coats, all three sweaters, one of the dresses, one of the pairs of tights, and her headband.

"That was my best headband," she said sadly, watching Emma walk away with it.

When the bell rang, the second-graders swarmed into Ms. Aruba-Tate's classroom. They were happy because it was time for Measuring. Measuring was a blast. Every kid got a plastic tape measure and a partner, and then they ran around like crazy, trying to measure things faster than everyone else. Ivy and Bean measured their heads and their fingers and their feet and their eyeballs and

their necks and their chair-legs and their pencils and the distance between the rug and the wall. Then they ran to their table and plopped themselves down in their chairs. "We finished first!" yelled Bean. "We win!"

Dusit and Drew plopped themselves down, too. "We finished second!"

"This is not a contest, friends," said Ms. Aruba-Tate. Sure it was! And Ivy and Bean had won! They smiled at each other.

After Measuring came Graphing. Graphing was not a blast. Graphing was a bummer.

Graphing was when you put all your measurements on a chart. You had to get all your numbers in the right place. You had to put the right-sized lines next to your numbers. You had to spell all your words right. You had to do everything right. Ivy was much better at things that had to be right than Bean was, so Bean let her be in charge of Graphing. Bean was in charge of keeping Ivy company and offering good suggestions, but that still gave her plenty of time to look around the room and think.

First she thought that Eric was using the same color green for two different lines. She pointed this out. He changed greens.

Then she thought that MacAdam couldn't have a 20-inch finger. Nobody had a 20-inch finger. She pointed this out. He ignored her.

Bean looked over at Zuzu and Vanessa's Graphing chart. They had done it all in different shades of pink. Vanessa had drawn flowers around the word "Graphing." It looked good.

Bean remembered something.

"Hey, Vanessa!" she hissed. "Ivy isn't spoiled. She gave away all her clothes."

"She can still be spoiled," said Vanessa.

"No!" said Bean. "Giving stuff away is the opposite of being spoiled!"

Vanessa shook her head.

"Ms. Aruba-Tate!" cried Bean. "You can't be spoiled if you give away all your clothes and your best headband, can you?"

Ms. Aruba-Tate looked up from her whiteboard. She frowned. "Who has given away all her clothes and her best headband?"

Nobody said anything. But they all looked at Ivy.

Graphing was even more of a bummer after that.

+ + + + + +

Ivy and Bean trailed slowly home. Bean was
slow because she was carrying all the clothes
that Ivy had had to take back. They were
heavy. She was surprised Ivy had been able to

walk at all that morning. Ivy was slow because she felt bad. Her face wasn't red anymore, but she still felt bad.

"I'm sorry I got you in trouble," Bean said again. "I wish I hadn't said anything."

"I know," sighed Ivy. "But now Ms. Aruba-Tate is mad at me."

"I don't get it. They tell you seven million times to share stuff," Bean said. "And then they freak out when you do it." She dropped a sweater. "Can you pick that up?"

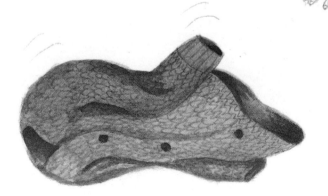

Ivy picked it up. "Yeah. Maybe she thought I was showing off." She started blinking hard. "Spoiled kids show off."

"I don't think you're spoiled," argued Bean.

"But what if I am?" Ivy asked. She looked worried. "Ms. Aruba-Tate thinks I am."

"No, she doesn't," said Bean. She thought about Ms. Aruba-Tate's frown. "I'm pretty sure she doesn't."

Ivy blinked some more. "I need to get unspoiled," she said. "For real."

"Okay," said Bean. "Don't worry. It's Friday. We've got the whole weekend to unspoil you."

HELP MUH!

On Saturday, Bean was unfortunately being swallowed by quicksand. First her feet—*slurp!*—and then her legs—*slurp!*—and then her middle—*slurp!* Inch by inch, she was sucked to her doom.

It was a tragic scene.

Nancy came into the living room and unrolled her yoga mat.

Bean struggled for survival.

Nancy held her leg behind her back.

Oh no! The quicksand was up to Bean's shoulders! It was just a matter of time.

Nancy held her other leg behind her back.

Bean was a goner.

Nancy bent in half until her head touched her knees.

But wait! Where there was life, there was hope! Bean used the last of her strength to leap to freedom.

Good golly, what a leap! The tips of her fingers scraped the edge of a nearby raft. She would be saved, if only she could stretch just a little farther, like this: *Eeeeeeep!*

Her fingers closed around the life-giving raft. She was saved!

"Get your grubby hands off my yoga mat!" puffed Nancy, upside down.

"Wa-tuh! Wa-tuh!" croaked Bean. Now she was dying of thirst. It was just one thing after another out here in the jungle. "Help muh!" Muh was the same thing as me, only sadder.

"Go away!" Nancy huffed.

Bean groaned.

Nancy fell over. "Bean! That was a perfect downward-dog and you ruined it. Mom! Bean's driving me bonkers!"

"Stop doing whatever you're doing, Bean," called their mom from another room.

"Okay!" yelled Bean. What a good kid she was! She was so good, she decided to help Nancy. "You know, that doesn't look anything like a dog," Bean said helpfully. "I think you're doing it wrong. Here's a dog." She got on her hands and knees and panted. "A-yerp! A-yerp, yerp, yerp!"

Nancy fell over again. "STOP MESSING ME UP! LEAVE ME ALONE!"

Bean stopped barking. "I thought yoga was supposed to make you calm."

"MO-OMM!" bellowed Nancy. She rushed out of the room.

Sheesh. Bean rolled onto Nancy's yoga mat and lay there. At least someone around here was calm.

"Bean!" There was Bean's mom. She seemed to be frowning. "If you can't leave Nancy alone, you'll have to go outside until she's done." She glared some more. "Can you leave Nancy alone?"

A trick question if Bean had ever heard one. "It's my house, too," she began.

"Out you go!" said her mom, pointing to the backyard.

"What?" yelped Bean. "I was helping Nancy. And I was here first!"

"Outside, Bean," said her mother, still pointing.

"You guys are ganging up on me! Two against one! It's not fair!" huffed Bean.

"Who said life was fair?" asked Bean's mom.

+ + + + + +

"Blame it on Bean!" huffed Bean. "That's the motto of this family!" She thumped down on the back steps. "There I am, lying on the floor, minding my own business, and all of a sudden, Nancy comes in, and bing bang bong, Bean's a criminal!" Bean turned toward the house and yelled (but not very loud), "Just because she's older doesn't make her right!" Then she slapped the step with her hand—*ow!*—and wished for the millionth time that she wasn't a little sister.

"Bean! Are you there?" It was Ivy, on the other side of the fence.

"Ivy! Come on in, old buddy, old pal!" yelled Bean. Just in the nick of time! A friend!

Ivy came charging through the gate. "I've got it! The cure!"

"For what?" asked Bean.

"For being spoiled! What do you think?" Ivy said.

"Oh, sorry. I forgot," said Bean.

"Jeez. If you were spoiled, I wouldn't forget," said Ivy. "I spent the whole morning working on it. At first, the only thing I could think of was giving you all my toys—"

"Really?" interrupted Bean. "Even the jiggly man?" The jiggly man was Ivy's best toy. He was a little gummy blue guy that you threw at the wall. He stuck there for a second and then he somersaulted—*bloop, bloop, bloop*—down the wall, leaving greasy marks where he had been. Bean loved him.

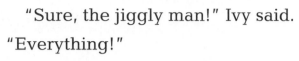

"Sure, the jiggly man!" Ivy said. "Everything!"

"Sounds good," said Bean. "I'll take 'em!"

"But then I thought, No, I'd get in trouble if I did that, just like I got in trouble for giving away my clothes."

"Oh." Bean was disappointed. "What if you only gave me the jiggly man?"

"No, because then I got a better idea." Ivy's eyes were shining. "Remember how Vanessa said that being an only child makes you spoiled? Remember?"

"Yeah," said Bean slowly, "but I don't think she's right about that."

Ivy ignored her. "So the cure is simple! All I have to do to get unspoiled is stop being an only child! I have to get a sister!"

THE ROAD TO DISASTERVILLE

Bean tried to warn her. Sisters were no good. They tattled on you if you did the tiniest thing a little bit wrong, and then you had to go sit outside. They bossed you. They got mad if you took one measly glass animal out of their rooms. They laughed at you. They completely freaked out about small problems, even if you were just about to clean them up. They told you your drawings were weird looking, your hair smelled, and there was a big scary secret that no one would ever tell you, not in a million years.

And then they smiled at you in a grown-uppy way, just to remind you that they knew it and you didn't. All day long, sisters did that. And then, right before bed, they said, "I was just kidding."

Ivy said that was older sisters. Younger sisters weren't like that. Younger sisters were perfectly okay. Especially very small ones. A baby sister, for instance, would be only half as annoying as Nancy, maybe even less. Just annoying enough to keep Ivy from getting spoiled.

A baby sister was what she needed.

"Trust me, you don't," said Bean.

"I do!" said Ivy.

Bean shook her head. "Next stop, Disasterville."

But Ivy was already zipping toward the gate. She stopped and looked back at Bean. "Come on!" she said. "Let's go tell my mom."

"Tell her what?" said Bean, getting up.

"Tell her to have a baby."

Wow. Bean didn't know how that was going to work, but she was interested to find out. Once she was at Ivy's house, though, she decided it would be more polite to wait in Ivy's room during the telling part.

It didn't take very long. Three minutes, maybe.

"What did she say?" asked Bean.

"She said HA!" Ivy answered, flopping down on her bed. "And then she sang a song about the old gray mare just ain't what she used to be. And then she said Absolutely not, no with a capital *N*."

"Sounds like she means it," said Bean. "You'd better just give me the jiggly man."

"No," said Ivy. "I'm going to brainstorm." Ms. Aruba-Tate was nuts about brainstorming. She was always doing it. When she brainstormed, Ms. Aruba-Tate wrote down words and drew circles around them with her big purple pen. She called this an Idea Map. Bean didn't really get why brainstorming was different than regular thinking, so she just watched while Ivy brainstormed. First, Ivy slid to the floor. Then, she put her hands over her eyes. After that, she rolled around and grunted.

It wasn't very interesting, watching Ivy brainstorm. Bean wandered over to Ivy's doll tenement. Ivy's room was divided into five little sections. There was an art studio, a sleeping area, a living room, a magic lab, and a doll tenement, where all of Ivy's dolls lived. Ivy had scads of dolls. She had regular plastic dolls, china dolls dressed like old-fashioned girls, dolls in fancy costumes, wooden dolls, stuffed dolls, Barbies, and even a rock in a nightgown. Bean poked around, looking for the jiggly man.

Ivy stopped rolling around the floor and put her feet up on the wall. That way the blood would slosh to her brain and make it storm.

Bean lifted the rock. No jiggly man. She peeked inside a doll-bed. "Ew," she said. "This one's gross." She held up a doll by its foot.

Ivy glanced up from the floor. "That's Zellaphine. She's supposed to look like a real baby."

She did. Zellaphine had blobby arms and legs. She had droopy fat cheeks and shiny drooly lips. In between her drooly lips, there was a little hole where you were supposed to stick a bottle. On her bald head was a pink knitted cap and on her squishy bottom was a big diaper. She gave Bean the creeps. "Let's bury her alive."

Ivy giggled. "Okay. When I'm done brainstorming."

"Well, hurry up," said Bean.

Ivy tried. How can I get a sister, she asked herself. How? How? She bugged her eyes out at the electrical outlet on her wall. Suddenly, her brain stormed. "Hey!" she said. "Electricity!"

"What about it?" said Bean. She waved Zellaphine. "Come on, let's bury her."

"No," said Ivy. "Let's put some electricity in her and make her come to life."

Ivy had seen it in a movie. "There was this guy who made a giant robot, and then he struck it with lightning, and it sat up," Ivy explained. "That's what we're going to do with Zellaphine."

Bean looked at Zellaphine's drooly lips and imagined her alive. Yuck. "Where are we going to get the lightning?"

"The guy in the movie had to use lightning because it was a long time ago and that was the only electricity he could get," Ivy said. "But now we have plugs." She pointed to the outlet. "We'll plug her in and charge her up."

Bean had a feeling it wouldn't work, but if it did, Ivy was going to be in big trouble. "You're going to have to change her diapers, you know."

"No way," said Ivy. "That's a mom-thing."

"You should ask your mom first, then."

Ivy went downstairs to talk to her mom and came back a few minutes later, holding a plug. "My mom says that if I make Zellaphine come alive with electricity, she will be happy to change her diapers because she supports scientific progress. She even gave me her phone plug for the charging."

One end of Ivy's mom's plug was a regular plug, but the other end was shaped like a tiny straw. It was easy to jam it into the hole where Zellaphine's bottle was supposed to go. Bean had wanted to stick it right into the top of Zellaphine's head, but Ivy thought it would be mean to make Zellaphine come alive with a hole in the top of her head. "See? I'm getting less spoiled already!" she said.

In the movie, the robot came to life on a special table, so Ivy and Bean laid Zellaphine

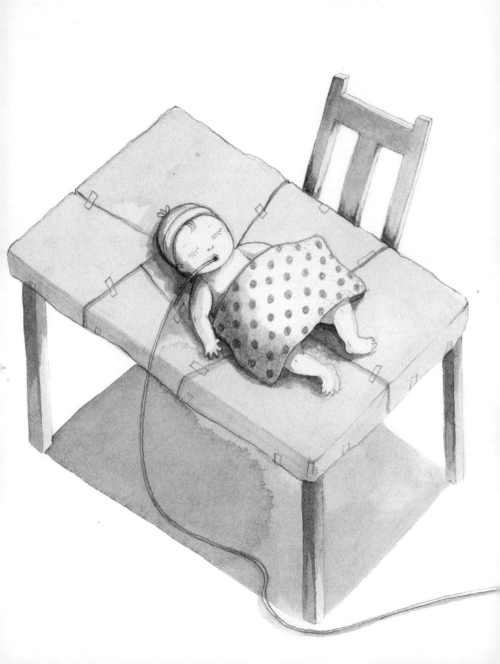

out on the table in Ivy's magic lab. The table was covered with tinfoil, so that it looked like a real lab table. Also so that it wouldn't get ruined when glop spilled on it.

Zellaphine's eyes closed when they laid her down. With her closed eyes and her drooly lips and her droopy cheeks, she looked like a real sleeping baby. A real sleeping baby with a plug in her mouth.

"We should put a blanket on her," said Bean. "Babies always have blankets."

They covered her with a blanket. Okay. Now they were ready. They decided to plug the other end of the cord into the electrical outlet together, so if Zellaphine did come to life, they would both be famous. Together, they crouched by the outlet. Together, they held the plug. Together, they said, "One."

"Two."

"Three."

"Plug!"

IN A PIGGLE

"I think I saw her arm move!" said Bean. Really, she hadn't seen anything, but pretending made life more interesting.

"I think I saw her breathe!" said Ivy. She made binoculars with her fingers and peered at Zellaphine. "The blanket's going up and down!"

"Waah," said Bean quietly out of the side of her mouth.

"That was you," Ivy giggled.

Bean tiptoed closer. Zellaphine lay like a blob on the tinfoil table. Her lips were still drooly. Her cheeks were still droopy. She wasn't moving.

"Maybe she's stunned," said Bean.

"Maybe," said Ivy. She looked at Zellaphine a moment and then she bonked her on the head. "Wake up, sister!"

"She'll thank us in the end!" Bean said. She picked

Zellaphine up and dropped her on the floor. "Wake up, baby!"

They threw Zellaphine around the room a little, but she didn't come to life. She was still a doll.

Bean thought it had been fun trying, but Ivy was worried. "I can feel myself getting more spoiled," she said.

"All you have to do is give me the jiggly man," said Bean. "Then you'll be cured."

Ivy shook her head. "No. I won't. That's how spoiled

I am. I won't give you the only toy you want. I won't even let you play with it."

"Aw, come on!" Suddenly, Bean wanted the jiggly man with all her heart. "Don't be so spoiled."

"See what I mean?" said Ivy. She chewed her thumb knuckle, which was a thing she did when she was worried. "I've got to get a sister."

"Let's try brain food," Bean suggested. Brain food was one of Bean and Ivy's greatest inventions. Everyone knows that food helps your brain think. But normal food just helps your brain think normal thoughts. When Ivy and Bean wanted to think un-normal thoughts, they ate un-normal food. That's why they called it brain food.

In the kitchen, Ivy got out carrot sticks and chocolate milk powder. One of the things

that Bean liked best about Ivy's house was chocolate milk powder. They each rolled a carrot in chocolate milk powder and chomped it down. "Dee-licious!" said Bean.

The second one wasn't quite as delicious. The third one was pretty bad.

"I think we need to try something else, anyway," said Ivy. "My thoughts are still normal." She rooted around in the refrigerator and found some pickles.

"That's good," Bean said. "Pickles are shaped like brains."

Slowly, Ivy peeled two bananas. She took a pickle in one hand and a banana in the other. So did Bean. "Go," said Ivy. She stuffed some banana in her mouth and took a bite of pickle. "Mm," she said, but she shivered when she said it.

Bean did it the other way around. She chomped off a big piece of pickle and shoved some banana in after it. "Wg," she said, swallowing.

Ivy's face shriveled as she took another bite of pickle.

"I think I'm starting to have un-normal thoughts," said Bean. She took a deep breath and ate half a banana.

"Puppapiginnere," said Ivy, which meant, Put a pickle in there. Her mouth was full.

Bean took a little bite of pickle. "Buh," she said.

Ivy's mom came into the kitchen. "What are you eating?" she asked.

"Pigglenana," said Ivy, shivering. She swallowed hard.

"Pickles and bananas," explained Bean. "It's helping us think un-normal thoughts."

"You two have plenty of un-normal thoughts already," said Ivy's mom.

"No," said Ivy. "We haven't even had one yet. I'm going to eat ten more and see what happens."

"I don't want to see what happens," said Ivy's mom sternly. "You may have one more."

"That's not going to be enough," said Ivy. She reached into the jar and pulled out the biggest pickle she could find. It was some pickle. It really looked like a brain. Ivy opened her mouth. But she didn't put the pickle in it.

"Eat up," said Bean, passing her a banana.

"Wait. I'm reading this pickle jar," said Ivy. And she was. She read it very slowly. On the front, it said "Barney's Extra Sour Dills, Pickles of the Gods." Then there was a picture of a lot of gods, sitting on a cloud, eating pickles. The most important god had a little balloon of words coming out of his mouth. "This is one fine pickle!"

THIS IS ONE FINE PICKLE!

"Just yam it down," said Bean. "Don't think about it."

Ivy put the pickle and the banana down. "I don't need to eat it. I just got a great idea."

"Good, because I feel gross," said Bean. The only thing brain food was making her think about was bananas. "What is it?"

Ivy couldn't wink, but she could cross her eyes big-time. She crossed her eyes at Bean, which meant, I can't tell you in front of my mom. "Let's go outside," she suggested. "With Zellaphine."

Ivy waited until they were in the front yard before she turned to Bean and whispered, "We need to beg the gods for a baby!"

ASKING FOR TROUBLE

Begging the gods for a baby turned out to be complicated. First, you had to find a spot with grass but without trees. If the gods dropped a baby out of the sky, you didn't want the baby getting stuck in a tree.

Ivy's backyard had too many rocks. Her front yard had too many scratchy bushes. Bean's front yard had trees. Her backyard? No way. A baby could get hurt on all the stuff in Bean's backyard.

In the end, they decided to go to Monkey Park, a block and a half from Pancake Court.

Now that Ivy and Bean were seven and nine-twelfths, they could go to Monkey Park by themselves, as long as they followed five million rules when they did it.

In Monkey Park were one big flat field and one not-so-flat field. Usually, the flat field was covered with soccer-playing kids, but now, in the middle of the afternoon, there were only a few kids there, kicking balls around. Which made it a perfect place to ask the gods for a baby. They could drop her anywhere and that baby would be fine.

"Okay," said Ivy, slapping her hands together. "The first thing we need to do is make a big circle of flowers."

"How do you know?" asked Bean.

"I've done this before," Ivy said. "I begged the gods for a kitten."

"Did it work?"

Ivy frowned. "Sort of. I got a stuffed kitten."

So it didn't work, Bean thought. But she didn't say that because she didn't want

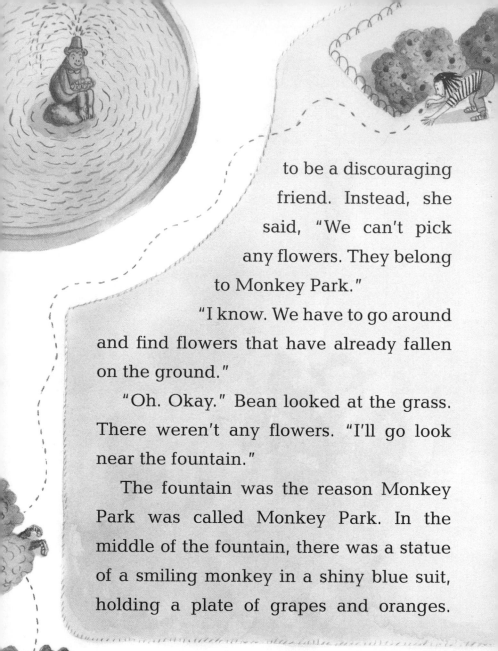

to be a discouraging friend. Instead, she said, "We can't pick any flowers. They belong to Monkey Park."

"I know. We have to go around and find flowers that have already fallen on the ground."

"Oh. Okay." Bean looked at the grass. There weren't any flowers. "I'll go look near the fountain."

The fountain was the reason Monkey Park was called Monkey Park. In the middle of the fountain, there was a statue of a smiling monkey in a shiny blue suit, holding a plate of grapes and oranges.

Water spurted out of his hat. As Bean walked around the fountain looking under bushes, she saw her neighbors, Jean the boy and Jean the girl, and their baby, Kalia. They were having a picnic.

"Hi, Bean!" called Jean the girl. "Whatcha doing?"

"Looking for dead flowers," said Bean. She found a petal and picked it up.

"You want some lunch?" asked Jean the boy. "We have pâté."

Pâté? Bean didn't know what it was, but it sounded terrible. Even worse than bananas and pickles. Bean didn't say that. She said, "Thanks, but I already had lunch a while ago."

Jean the boy looked grumpy. "We were supposed to have lunch a while ago, but somebody needed a nap." He squinted at Kalia, who had brown goop smeared all over her face.

"No!" said Kalia.

"And then somebody yelled for an hour and a half," added Jean the girl, squinting at Kalia, too.

"Nono!" said Kalia.

"And then somebody had a big poop," said Jean the boy.

"NO!" hollered Kalia. She staggered toward Bean with her goopy brown hands. "BEEBEE!"

Bean waved and zipped away as fast as she could. She poked under bushes until she found some purple flowers and some pink flowers and some white flowers and some

flowers that were so dead they were brown.
When she brought them back to the flat field,
Ivy used almost all of them to make a giant
circle. The rest she handed to Bean.

"Okay," Ivy said.
"I'll stand in the middle
of the circle with Zellaphine
and do the begging,
while you dance
around the edge
of the circle and toss
flowers."

"Dance around the edge of the circle and toss flowers?" asked Bean. "Me? Why?"

"Gods like it," said Ivy firmly.

"What are you going to be doing?"

"I'm going to be chanting. Also throwing Zellaphine up in the air, so they get the right idea. With the gods, you have to be really clear."

Chanting and throwing Zellaphine around sounded better than dancing in a circle and tossing flowers. "Why can't I do the chanting part?" asked Bean.

"I'm the one who needs the sister," said Ivy. "I have to do the chanting." She stepped into the center of the circle and held Zellaphine up to the sky. "Ooooo!" she cried. Then she looked over her shoulder at Bean. "Dance!" she whispered.

Bean hopped from one foot to the other. She felt dumb.

"I seek your help because I'm getting spoiled down here!" yelled Ivy. She waved Zellaphine at the sky. "I need one of these! Only real!"

Bean hopped from her second foot back to her first foot. She tossed a couple of flowers. The kids on the other side of the field stopped kicking balls to watch. Bean wished the gods would hurry up.

"Yoooo-hooooo!" yelled Ivy. "Take this offering!" She threw Zellaphine into the sky. "And give me a sister!" She looked over her shoulder. "Dance harder."

Bean did a kick.

The watching kids laughed.

Bean scowled at them. Stupid gods, she thought. Stupid baby.

Ivy closed her eyes and yelled, "I'm not even watching, gods, so don't worry that I'll see you!" Nothing happened. "Dance!" she hissed.

Bean skipped. So did the watching kids.

"If you need a few minutes to find one, I can wait!" Ivy called to the sky. "Oh gods!" She held out her arms, ready to catch a baby. "I'll be right here! Ready when you are!"

The watching kids held out their arms and staggered around.

And suddenly Bean had a wonderful idea.

MIRACLE IN MONKEY PARK

Bean tore through Monkey Park and skidded to a halt in front of Jean and Jean. "Can I borrow Kalia?" she panted.

"NO!" said Kalia.

"Sure!" said Jean and Jean.

"I'll bring her back soon," Bean promised. She took Kalia by the goopy hand. "Come on! This is going to be fun!"

"Take your time!" called Jean the boy as Bean and Kalia took off. "Keep her as long as you want!"

Bean soon learned that Kalia couldn't run like a normal person. Her legs were too short, for one thing. For another, she couldn't concentrate. She kept falling over. Finally, Bean was forced to pick her up. The goopy brown smears were even more disgusting close up. Also, she smelled. "You smell," said Bean. "NO!" said Kalia. She hugged Bean.

"Ew," said Bean, but she didn't have time to argue. She had to hurry.

And she made it! Ivy was still begging with her eyes closed and her arms out. The watching kids had gotten bored. They had gone back to kicking balls.

"Oh ye gods, save me!" Ivy chanted. "Give me a baby sister!" She wiggled her fingers to show that she was ready to catch a baby.

Bean put her hand over Kalia's smeary mouth and tiptoed into the circle just as Ivy finished up a long "Ooooooh gods!" Quickly, Bean rolled Kalia right into Ivy's open arms. Ivy's eyes flew open. "Yikes!" she squawked.

"Holy moly cannoli, your prayers have been answered, Ivy!" cried Bean. "You've got yourself a fine baby sister!"

"Wow." Ivy stared at Kalia's smeary face. "Isn't this Kalia?"

"BEEBEE!" hollered Kalia, twisting around to find Bean.

"Nope. Not Kalia. This one dropped right out of the sky," said Bean in an excited voice. "I saw the whole thing!"

"NONONO!" wailed Kalia, reaching for Bean.

Ivy looked doubtfully at Bean. Bean opened her eyes as wide as they would go. "It's a miracle."

Ivy giggled. Then she gave Kalia a big hug and cried, "My darling sister!" She made a face. "Pew."

"NONO!" Kalia kicked her legs and slid down Ivy to get to the ground. Then she ran for Bean. "My BEEBEE!"

"Sorry, Charlie," said Bean, turning her around. "Go to sister."

"No! BeeBee." Kalia stuffed some of Bean's pants into her mouth.

"Here, sister!" called Ivy. "I have a doll for you." She picked Zellaphine up off the ground and waved her at Kalia. "Dolly, dolly!"

Kalia looked at Zellaphine for a moment. Then she snatched the doll and hit Ivy with it. "NO!"

"Ow," said Ivy, rubbing her leg where Zellaphine hit it.

"This is what it's like," said Bean. "I tried to warn you."

Ivy shook her head. "I think the gods must have been trying to get rid of this one."

"Beggars can't be choosers," said Bean. "You'll be unspoiled in a jiffy."

Ivy looked at Kalia. "What exactly do you do with babies?"

Bean didn't really know what people did with babies, but she said, "You rock them to sleep."

Ivy watched Kalia bang Zellaphine's head in the dirt. "She doesn't look very sleepy."

"That's why you have to rock them," said Bean.

Ivy chased Kalia until she caught her.

She had to hold her pretty tight so she couldn't get away. Then she rocked. Rock, rock, rock.

"NONONONONONO!!!!" screamed Kalia. "MAMAMAMAMAMAM!"

Rock, rock, rock.

"MAMAMAMAMAM!!"

"Are you sure this is normal?" Ivy said, rocking.

"Totally normal," said Bean.

Kalia hit Ivy on the ear. "MAMAMAM!"

Ivy stopped rocking. "Hark!" she cried. "She's calling for her goddess-mother to come and get her."

"Nah," said Bean. "She's saying, Gosh, I love my new sister."

"No, she wants to go home," said Ivy. She put her hand to her ear. "And hark, I hear the voice of her goddess-mother, calling for her child."

"I don't hear anything," said Bean.

"She's saying, 'My baby, my baby!'" Ivy said. "If we offend the gods, we will be punished."

"Not me," said Bean. "I'm just sitting here."

Ivy sighed deeply. "Both of us. It is dangerous to anger the goddess." She looked lovingly at Kalia. "I must return you, darling sister, though it saddens my heart."

"MAM!"

"Hi, honey!" It was Jean the girl, coming down the path.

"See?" said Ivy. She opened her arms. "Go! Return to your mother."

Kalia burst out of Ivy's arms and ran like crazy. "MAMAMAMAMAM!"

"She returns to the gods," said Ivy. She looked sideways at Bean.

"There you are, bunny!" said Jean, scooping Kalia up. "Thanks for watching her, Bean!" she called. "And you too, Ivy!"

Ivy bowed. "The goddess speaks," she whispered.

"Anytime you girls want to borrow her again, you just let me know!" Jean cried.

Bean tried to look like she thought that was a good idea. "We sure will!"

"Not a chance," Ivy whispered.

NOT TOO BIG,
NOT TOO LITTLE

Ivy and Bean walked slowly back to Pancake Court. Finally, Ivy spoke. "You're right about baby sisters. They're terrible."

"Big sisters are worse," said Bean.

"If big ones are bad and little ones are bad, that doesn't leave much."

"There's twins," Bean said. "I always wished I was a twin. Think how cool it would be, like having a friend in your house. It would be like you and me, only sisters."

Ivy nodded. "But you can't get a twin. You have to be born that way."

"Wouldn't it be great?" said Bean dreamily. "You could gang up on your older sister."

Ivy frowned. "I don't have an older sister."

"But if you did, and you had a twin, you could gang up on her. You'd be able to play with her stuff. And for once in your life you might win an argument." Bean thought some more. "Plus, it would be fun. If you and I were twins, we'd get to play all the time and every night would be like a sleepover."

"Except we wouldn't be us," said Ivy. "Because we wouldn't have our parents."

Bean shrugged. "It wouldn't matter! We'd have each other!"

Ivy thought about that. "Yeah. But it's too late. We're not twins."

"Life isn't fair," said Bean gloomily.

+ + + + + +

But that night, Bean had an amazing idea.
It was an idea that would
fix Ivy's spoilment and
life's unfairness at the
same time. It was an idea
that would make everything
better. Plus it was an idea
that didn't need gods or
electricity or magic to work.
All it needed was nature.

Here's how Bean's idea went: Kids grow. Everyone knows that. All the time, they're growing and growing. They get taller. Their feet get bigger. Even their heads grow, which is weird but true. What's covering all these growing parts? Skin, that's what! And what does that mean about skin? It's growing, too! All the time!

So, let's say you wanted to be a twin. Let's say you wanted to be a twin with your friend. All you would have to do is tie yourself to her with string and wait. After a while, your skins would grow together, and you would become twins.

Easy-peasy!

Bean wanted to go over to Ivy's house right that minute, to tell her the amazing idea. Bean's mom said Absolutely not and It's 10 P.M. and Why aren't you asleep?

"Okay, okay," grumped Bean, as she thumped back to her room. "But don't be surprised when you have to buy more food. And maybe a bigger bed, too."

Her mom looked confused. "What?"

"You'll see!"

+ + + + + +

"It's nature," explained Bean the next day, as she looped string around her arm and Ivy's. "Nature always works. We'll be twins! Ha! Nancy's going to freak!"

"And we won't just be regular twins," Ivy said. "We'll be the joined kind, which is the coolest. Tie that knot tight."

Originally, Bean had wanted to tape their heads together, so they'd be joined at the head, but Ivy had pointed out that they'd have to bend sideways for the rest of their lives. Plus, they'd have tape in their hair. Joined arms would be way easier. Bean had to admit this was true.

Bean tied the last knot. "Okay!" she said. "That should do it." She leaned back against the wall of her puny plastic playhouse, and Ivy leaned with her (she had to). "We'll be the three-arm twins!" After a moment, she

said, "I can kind of feel our skin growing together."

"Me too," said Ivy.

"How long do you think it'll take?"

"A month, maybe," said Ivy.

"A month!" yelped Bean. "That's a long time!"

"But in the end, we'll be joined forever," Ivy said. "Forever!"

"And then we're going to rule the world!" said Bean. "Ha!"

"You keep saying Ha," Ivy said.

"Let's go show people!" Bean was too excited to sit still.

"People?" Ivy said. "I'm reading this really great book—"

"You can read later," said Bean. "Maybe."

It was pretty hard for them to squeeze through the tiny door of Bean's playhouse, but finally Bean figured out that if she crawled backward and Ivy crawled forward, they could make it out. Still, their heads clonked together.

Nancy was sitting on her yoga mat on the other side of the lawn. One of her legs was crossed over the other and her head was turned the opposite way. "Don't talk," she said. "I'm doing yoga."

"Now you've taken over the backyard too?" said Bean. "That's not fair!" Ooh, she could hardly wait until she and Ivy grew together! Nancy wouldn't know what hit her! Bean couldn't help saying

in a mysterious voice, "Pretty soon, things are going to be different around here."

"Stop talking," said Nancy.

"I'm not talking to you," said Bean. "Even though your life is about to change forever and you probably won't like it."

Nancy crossed her legs in the other direction.

"Does the word 'twin' strike fear in your heart?" asked Bean.

"No," Nancy said. She opened her eyes and looked at Bean and Ivy. "Oh, good. You're stuck together. Does this mean you're going to move in with Ivy?"

"No!" said Bean. "Ivy's going to move in with me! So ha!"

Ivy frowned. "I thought we were going to switch off," she said.

Bean looked at her in surprise. "The plan was to move to my house."

Ivy shook her head. "You didn't say that before. You said it didn't matter."

Nancy made praying hands and lifted her face to the sky. "You two are only going to be half as annoying with one arm each."

Bean looked at Nancy. Then she looked at her tied-up arm. "Let's get out of here," she said to Ivy.

A KNOTTY PROBLEM

For a while, Ivy and Bean sat in Bean's driveway. Then Bean said, "Let's go show our arm to Dino." Maybe it would strike fear in his heart.

But it didn't, because Dino wasn't home. Dino's mom answered the doorbell. She had one pair of glasses on her head and one on her eyes. "What happened to you two?" she asked, squinting at their tied-up arm.

Bean always thought it was better not to tell grown-ups exactly what was going on, but Ivy answered right away. "We're making ourselves into twins by growing our skin together."

Dino's mom took the pair of glasses on her head and put them over the glasses on her eyes to take a closer look. "What a good idea. Whose house are you going to live in once you're done?"

"Mine," said Bean.

"We're going to switch off," said Ivy.

Bean wished Ivy would stop saying that.

She liked her own house. That's where her mom and dad were. Unfortunately, Nancy was there, too. But still. All her stuff was there. She decided to change the subject. "Where's Dino?" she asked.

"He's over at Sophie W.'s, playing bannis," said Dino's mom.

Bannis! Bannis was a famous Pancake Court game. It was baseball played with a tennis ball. Dino and Bean and Liana had thought it up after Liana broke a window with a softball. You almost never broke a window in bannis, partly because tennis balls were soft and partly because in bannis, the bat was a bamboo stick. You hardly ever hit the ball, and if you did, the stick usually broke. Bean loved bannis. She loved whacking the tennis ball as hard as she could and then

throwing the broken stick on the ground. Sometimes she spit in the dirt, too, just for good measure.

But now she was a twin.

You couldn't play bannis with one arm tied to another person. Especially if that person was Ivy. Ivy couldn't hit things with sticks. Ivy didn't even like hitting things with sticks. Ivy liked reading books.

Bean imagined herself, sitting in a chair with Ivy while she read a book, for an hour.

She imagined Ivy's mom kissing her goodnight.

She imagined never, ever playing bannis again.

Yikes! Her life wasn't getting better. It was getting worse. Bean and Ivy said goodbye to Dino's mom and went to sit on the grass.

"So this is being a twin," said Bean.

They were both quiet for a long time.

BLOOP, BLOOP, BLOOP

"You know," said Ivy at last, "I don't think we should do this." She wiggled their arm.

"What? How come?" asked Bean. She tried to sound disappointed.

"It's mean to our parents," explained Ivy. "If it works, they'll be really sad when we're at the other person's house. Especially my mom. At least your parents have Nancy."

"But that's Nancy," said Bean. "My parents would miss me a lot."

Ivy nodded. "We have to think of other people."

Bean nodded, too. "We have to be unselfish. Nancy would be way worse without me around."

"Even though it would be great for us," said Ivy.

Bean's knot was so good they couldn't untie it. They had to chew it. First Bean chewed, and then Ivy chewed. Finally, with one big chew, Bean bit through the string, and they each had two arms again.

"Darn!" said Bean, waving her arm around. "No more twin!"

"And I'm still spoiled," said Ivy, waving her arm around.

Bean stopped waving her arm. "You know, Ivy, if you were spoiled, you wouldn't have thought of our parents. You would only have thought of yourself."

"Hmm." Ivy thought about that.

"You never did seem very spoiled to me," said Bean.

"Maybe I don't really need a sister," said Ivy.

"Right! Sisters are nothing but trouble."

"Especially that Kalia," said Ivy. "Pew!"

"All right then! I'm going to play some bannis!" Bean said, swinging an imaginary bamboo stick.

"I'm going to read," said Ivy.

"You're a big weirdo," said Bean.

"No, you're a big weirdo," said Ivy. "See you!"

"See you!"

Off they ran, in different directions.

+ + + + + +

Bean broke two bamboo sticks, playing bannis. She spit in the dirt, too. After that, she went home and did her regular things, like eating dinner and both wanting and not wanting to take a bath, and going to sleep. She forgot all about sisters and twins and spoiledness until the next day at school, during lunch, when Ivy looked in her lunchbox and said, "Oh. Here." She pulled out the jiggly man and threw him to Bean. "You can have him."

Bean looked at his little gummy blue body. "For real? Forever?"

Ivy nodded.

"You are not spoiled at all!" Bean said, jumping to her feet. She raced to the nearest wall and threw the jiggly man at it. Splat! He hung there for a moment. Then—*bloop, bloop, bloop*—down the wall he went.

Eric popped up next to her. "Ew, is he made out of boogers?"

"Yep," said Bean.
"Blue boogers."

"Let me try!"

Generously, Bean let Eric throw the jiggly man. Splat! *Bloop, bloop, bloop.* Then Leo wanted to try. Then Emma. Then Marga-Lee. *Bloop, bloop, bloop, bloop, bloop.* . . . Pretty soon, there was a line of kids waiting to throw him against the wall.

Bloop, bloop, bloop. "I want one of these guys," said Dusit, handing the jiggly man back to Bean. "Where'd you get him?"

"Ivy gave him to me," said Bean.

"My turn," said Vanessa, holding out her hand.

Bean hesitated. "Pretty nice of
Ivy to give him to me, huh?"

"Yeah, yeah," said Vanessa, still holding out her hand.

"Pretty unspoiled, don't you think?" asked Bean. "I mean, a spoiled kid would never do something like that, right?" She looked at Vanessa.

Vanessa looked at the jiggly man. "Right," she said.

That was good enough for Bean. She handed the gummy blue guy to Vanessa. "Here you go! Give him a good splat!"

Bloop,

bloop,

bloop.